A Templar Book

Produced by The Templar Company plc,
Pippbrook Mill, London Road, Dorking, Surrey RH4 1JE, Great Britain.

This edition produced for Parragon Books,
Unit 13-17, Avonbridge Trading Estate, Atlantic Road, Avonmouth, Bristol BS11 9QD

This book contains material first published as
Dickie and the West Wind in Enid Blyton's Sunny Stories
and Sunny Stories between 1926 and 1953.

Illustrated by Maggie Downer

Printed and bound in Italy

ISBN 1 85813 538 9

Enid Blyton's

POCKET LIBRARY

BILLY AND THE WEST WIND

Illustrated by Maggie Downer

PARRAGON

Billy's mother was very unhappy. When Billy
came home from school she had tears in her
eyes and she was hunting all over the place
for something.

"What's the matter, Mummy?"
asked Billy in surprise, for he thought
that grown-ups never cried.

"I've lost my lovely diamond ring,"
said his mother. "It's the one your
daddy gave me years ago, and I love
it best of all my rings. It was loose
and it must have dropped off.
Now I can't find it anywhere,
and I'm so unhappy
about it."

"I'll help you to look for it," said
Billy, at once. "Just tell me all the
places you've been this morning,
Mummy."

"I had it on at breakfast-time,"
said his mother. "Then I went
to see old Mrs. Brown who
lives at the far edge of the
meadow. I may have
dropped it on my way
there, of course.
Perhaps you'd like
to go and look on
the path, Billy."

So off Billy ran, his eyes looking all over the ground as he went. It was very windy, and the grass kept blowing about, which made it very difficult to see the ground properly. He soon came to the meadow and then he went down on his hands and knees and began to look very carefully indeed. He did so want to find that ring!

Suddenly he saw a small figure dart quickly behind a bush. It was too big for a rabbit and too small to be one of his playmates about to play a trick on him. What could it be? He peeped round the bush and what do you think he found, hiding there?

It was a small elf, with wide, frightened eyes and tiny, pointed ears! Now Billy had never in his life seen an elf and he stared in surprise.

"Please don't hurt me!"
said the elf, in a little
tinkling voice.
"Of course I won't!"
said Billy. "But where
are your wings? I
thought all elves had
wings and could fly."

"Well, I usually *do* have wings," said the little creature who was clothed in a beautiful suit of purple and blue. "They are lovely silver ones, and I took them off this morning to clean them. I put them down on that bush there, and the wind came along and blew them away. Now I'm looking everywhere for them, but I can't find them anywhere. It's too awful!"

"I'm looking for something too," said Billy. "I'm hunting for my mother's diamond ring. Have you seen it?"

"No," said the elf. "But I can easily get it for you, if you'll help me find my wings."

"Could you really?" said Billy, excitedly. "But how am I to help *you*?"

"You could go to the West Wind and ask him what he's done with my wings," said the elf. "I can't do it myself because I'm afraid of him – he's so big and blustery – but you are big and tall so perhaps you wouldn't mind."

"What an adventure this is turning out to be!" thought Billy to himself, feeling more and more excited.

"Of course I will help you," said Billy to the elf. "But wherever will I find the West Wind? I didn't even know it was a person!"

"Oh, goodness!" said the elf, laughing. "He's very much a person, I can tell you. He's gone to see his cousin, the Rainbow Lady, on the top of Blowaway Hill."

"Where's that?" asked Billy. "Tell me, and I'll go straight away."

"Well, the quickest way is to find the tower in the wood," said the elf, pointing down a little rabbit-path through some trees. "It has two doors. Go in the one that faces the sun. Shut it. Wish that you could be in the same place as the West Wind. Open the other door and you'll find yourself there! Then just ask the West Wind what he's done with my wings and tell him he really must let me have them back."

Billy waved goodbye and ran off down the narrow little path. He had never been down it before. After a while he came to a tall, thin tower amongst the trees. Billy walked all round it. It looked very strange indeed. There were no windows, but there were two small round doors. One faced the sun and the other was in shadow, just as the elf had described.

Billy opened the sunny door and walked boldly through. The tower was high, dark, and cold inside. Shivering, Billy shut the door behind him and found himself in black darkness, just like night! He felt a little frightened, but he remembered what the elf has said and shouted:

"I wish I was on the top of Blowaway Hill."

He heard a faint rushing sound and the tower rocked very slightly. Billy opened the other door and daylight streamed into the strange tower, making him blink. He walked out of the door – and *how* surprised he was!

He was no longer in the wood – he was on the top of a sunny hill, and in front of him was a small pretty cottage, overgrown with honeysuckle.

"This must be the Rainbow Lady's house," thought Billy. He marched up the little path and knocked at the door. A voice called "Come in!" So Billy turned the handle...

A draught of cold air blew on him as soon as he stepped inside. He shivered and looked round in surprise. Two people were sitting drinking lemonade at a little round table. A fire burned brightly in one corner and a grey cat sat washing itself on the rug. Everything seemed quite ordinary until he looked at the people there!

One was the Rainbow Lady. She was very beautiful and her dress was so bright that Billy blinked his eyes when he looked at her. She was dressed in all the colours of the rainbow, and her dress floated out around her like a mist. Her eyes shone like two stars.

The other person was the West Wind. He was fat and blustery, and his breath came in great gusts as if he had been running very hard. It was his breathing that made the big windy draughts that blew round the little room. His clothes were like April clouds and blew out round him all the time. Billy was so astonished to see him that at first he couldn't say a word.

"Well! What do you want?" asked the West Wind in a gusty voice. As he spoke Billy felt a shower of raindrops fall on him. It was very strange.

"I've come from the little elf who lives down in the meadow," said Billy. "She says you took away her wings this morning, West Wind, and she does so badly want them back."

"Dear me!" said the West Wind, surprised, and as he spoke another shower of raindrops fell on Billy's head. "How was I to know they belonged to the elf? I thought they had been put there by someone who didn't want them! I knew the red goblin was wanting a pair of wings so I blew them to him!"

"Oh dear!" said Billy, in dismay. "What a pity! The elf is really very upset. She can't fly, you see. She only took them off to clean them."

"West Wind, you are always doing silly things like that," said the Rainbow Lady, in a soft voice. "One day you will get into trouble. You had better go to the red goblin and ask for those wings back."

"Oh, no, I can't do that," said the West Wind, looking very uncomfortable and puffing more raindrops all over the room.

Billy looked round to see if there was an umbrella anywhere. It was not very nice to have showers of rain falling all over him whenever the West Wind spoke. He found an umbrella in a corner and put it up over himself.

"Oh, yes, you *can* go and get the wings back," said the Rainbow Lady, and she said it so firmly that the West Wind eventually agreed. He got up, took Billy's hand and went sulkily out of the door. He had a very cold, wet hand, but Billy didn't mind. It was very exciting.

The West Wind took Billy down the hill at such a pace that the little boy gasped for breath. They came to a river and the Wind jumped straight across it, dragging Billy with him. Then he rushed across some fields and at last came to a small, lop-sided house. A tiny goblin sat in the garden with a schoolbook, crying bitterly. The West Wind took no notice of the little creature but walked quickly up and knocked on the door.

"Stay here," he said to Billy, and left him in the garden. The little boy went over to the goblin.

"What's the matter?" he asked. The little goblin looked up. He had a quaint, pointed face and different coloured eyes – one was green and the other was yellow.

"I can't do my homework," he said. "Look! It's taking-away sums and this one *won't* take away."

Billy looked – and then he smiled – for the silly little goblin had put the sum down wrong! He had to take 18 from 81, and he had written the sum upside down so that he was trying to take 81 away from 18. No wonder it wouldn't come right!

Billy put the sum down right for him and the goblin did it easily. He was *so* grateful.

"Is there anything else I can help you with?" asked Billy kindly.

"Well," said the goblin shyly. "I never can remember which is my right hand and which is my left, and I'm always getting into dreadful trouble at school because of that. I suppose you can't tell me the best way to remember which hand is which?"

"Oh, that's easy!" said Billy at once. "The hand you are *writing* with is your *right* hand, and the one that's *left* is the *left* one, of course!"

"Oh, that's wonderful!" said the little goblin, in delight. "I shall never forget now. I always know which hand I write with, so I shall always know my *right* hand and the other one *must* be the left. Right hand, left hand, right hand, left hand!"

Just at that moment the door of the little house flew open and out came the West Wind in a fearful temper.

"That miserable red goblin won't give me back those wings!" he roared, and a whole shower of rain fell heavily on poor Billy and his new goblin friend. "So we can't have them!"

Billy stared in dismay. Now he wouldn't be able to take them to the elf and she wouldn't give him his mother's ring! It was too bad. He looked so upset that the small goblin he had just helped gently took hold of his hand.

"What's the matter?" he asked. "Do you want those silver wings that the West Wind gave my father this morning? They were really for me to learn to fly on, but if you badly want them, you shall have them back. You've been so kind to me! I'd like to do something in return!"

"Oh, *would* you let me have the wings!" said Billy, in delight. The little goblin said nothing but ran indoors. He came out with a pair of glittering silver wings and gave them to Billy. The little boy thanked him joyfully and turned to go. The West Wind took his hand and back they went to Blowaway Hill again.

·37·

"Well, you never know when a little kindness is going to bring you a big reward!" said the West Wind, in a jolly voice. "It's a good thing you helped that little goblin, isn't it?"

"Oh, yes," said Billy happily. "Now I must get back to the meadow again and give these wings to the elf."

But when he turned to look, he was dismayed to see that the tower had disappeared.

"Oh no!" he cried. "The tower has gone! However am I to get back home?"

Poor Billy! It was quite true – the magic tower had gone and could not take him back to the wood as he had planned! But luckily the Rainbow Lady was watching through the window and came out to see what was wrong.

"Don't worry," she said when Billy explained what had happened. "Just put on these elf wings, and the West Wind will blow you gently through the air back to the meadow."

The Rainbow Lady took the wings from Billy and clipped them neatly on to his shoulders.

"Now!" she said, turning to the West Wind. "I said GENTLY, so please don't be rough. Remember your manners for once!"

Then Billy felt himself rising into the air, higher and higher until he was far above the hill. His wings beat gently backwards and forwards and the West Wind blew him swiftly along. It was a most wonderful feeling.

"This is the most marvellous adventure I shall ever have!" said Billy, joyfully. "Oh, how I wish I always had wings! It is lovely to fly like this!"

The West Wind smiled and remembered his manners and did not blow too roughly. Soon Billy could see the meadow far below and the two of them started to glide gently downwards.

The West Wind said goodbye and left Billy on the edge of wood. He soon found a path he knew and ran along to the bush where he had seen the elf. She was still there waiting for him. When she saw that he had her wings on his back she cried out in delight and ran to meet him.

She unclipped her wings
from Billy's shoulders
and put them on her own.
"Oh, thank you, thank
you!" she cried.

"Could you give me my
mother's ring now?"
asked Billy. "You said you
would if I helped you."

BILLY AND THE WEST WIND

"Of course!" said the elf. "Whilst you were gone I set all the rabbits in the wood hunting for me – and one of them brought me this lovely shining ring. Is it your mother's?"

Of course, it was! So Billy ran all the way home and when he showed his mother the ring she could hardly believe her eyes.

"You *are* clever to find it!" she said.

"I didn't find it – a rabbit found it," said Billy. But his mother didn't believe him, and when he told her his adventure she said he really must have been dreaming!

So next week he is going to ask that elf to come to tea with him – and then everyone will know it wasn't a dream! I wish I was going for tea with them, too, don't you?